HANS CHRISTIAN ANDERSEN COULDN'T SPELL

and Other Fact & Fiction of the Famous

by
Nancy Polette

Illustrated by Jerry Warshaw

Printed in U.S.A.

P. O. Box 9450
O'Fallon, MO
63366

ISBN 0-913839-67-1

Book
Lures
Inc.

Contents | *Page*

FACT OR FICTION?

Hans Christian Andersen couldn't spell.

FACT !

As a child Hans listened to the strange tales told by the old fishwives and daydreamed about mermaids who fall in love with princes. He considered spelling and other rote learning dull and put forth little effort in school.

His daydreams, however, later became the stories for which he became famous and in each story Andersen always saw himself as the hero.

FACT OR FICTION?

Duke Ellington gave piano concerts at the age of seven.

FICTION !

As a child, Duke Ellington showed little interest in music. He loved to draw and learned to create moods with colors. As a teen he made a discovery which was to change his life! Music and art *both* have color and mood! Duke Ellington proved to be the first to bring the two together to create a new kind of music.

FACT OR FICTION?

Thomas Edison was a firebug.

FACT !

Curiosity killed the cat is an old saying. Curiosity can also get small boys into big trouble. That is what happened to young Tom when he burned down his father's barn just to see what a fire would do! "That boy is slow, dull-witted and nothing but trouble," his teachers moaned. Finally Tom's mother took him out of school and taught him at home. Here he was free to explore and experiment. Without this freedom to see "what would happen if", Tom might never have invented the electric light!

FACT OR FICTION?

Charles Dickens won the writing prize in grammar school.

FICTION !

Not only did Dickens not win prizes in school, he rarely saw the inside of a school. When he was nine, his father was taken to debtor's prison and Charles was sent to the dye factory to earn money to help feed the family. Day after day, pasting labels on blacking bottles, Charles dreamed dreams to escape the awful place. Years later those dreams became some of the world's best-loved novels, including OLIVER TWIST and DAVID COPPERFIELD.

FACT OR FICTION?

Charles Lindbergh was afraid of heights.

FACT !

When you are small, the world can be a scary place. Charles was afraid of two things: dark rooms and high places.

"He's a daydreamer, a loner, a terrible student," his teachers complained. But others noticed that he was never satisfied until he could discover *how* things worked. He always wanted to be first to try something new. Perhaps that is why he was the first to fly alone across the Atlantic Ocean even though he was afraid of heights!

FACT OR FICTION?

Louisa May Alcott wrote shocking books.

FACT !

The author of LITTLE WOMEN wrote her first novel at the age of twenty. It was an adult novel called MOODS and told of a woman who loved one man but married another. This was considered quite shocking in 1864 and the book did not do well.
Louisa May Alcott achieved her later success as a writer with the classics, LITTLE WOMEN and LITTLE MEN.

FACT OR FICTION?

Albert Einstein spoke his first word at the age of six months.

FICTION !

Einstein was *not* an early talker. In fact, he was nearly four years old before he spoke his first word. At age eighteen he was rejected from the Munich Institute of Technology because "he didn't show any promise." Not until late adult life did Einstein receive recognition as one of the world's great brains.

FACT OR FICTION?

Alexander Graham Bell never finished a project.

FACT !

Bell's wife was often heard to say, "He would be tinkering with the telephone yet if I hadn't taken it away from him."

This famous inventor was always more concerned with the search for new ideas than the final result of those ideas. Without others to push him to bringing projects to an end we might still be without the telephone!

FACT OR FICTION?

Abraham Lincoln entered the army as a captain and was discharged as a private.

FACT !

When Abraham Lincoln first enlisted in the army during the Black Hawk Wars, the men elected their leaders. Lincoln was elected captain. When it was time to enlist again, Lincoln automatically reverted to the rank of private; a rank he held when he left the army.

FACT OR FICTION?

Marie Curie's parents were delighted when she began reading at the age of three.

FICTION !

Marie Curie did begin reading at the age of three but her parents were *not* delighted. Their greatest fear was that friends and neighbors would discover that their child was "different". Even though books were kept from Marie, her mind soaked up all she heard. She became one of the discoverers of radium and a famed woman scientist.

FACT OR FICTION?

Grandma Moses never had an art lesson.

FACT !

For many years Anna Mary Moses had made stitchery pictures for her friends. When age slowed down her nimble fingers she decided that working with brushes and paint would be easier. She painted more than 1000 pictures, and all without a single art lesson.

FACT OR FICTION?

Louis Pasteur was an "A" student in science.

FICTION !

Pasteur was considered by most of his teachers to be a below average student. His slowness to answer when questioned irritated those who taught him. His father noticed, however, that while he took a long time to think about a problem that when he did figure it out he was usually right. This methodical mind was later in life to discover methods of vaccination for smallpox and pasteurization of milk.

FACT OR FICTION?

Winston Churchill failed the sixth grade.

FACT !

Winston Churchill, who became Prime Minister of Great Britain during World War II, was not a top student in school! One thing he was very good at was talking. He learned that he could easily dictate essays to other students who had trouble writing. In return they helped Winston with those subjects he cared little about. After repeating one grade he went on to do well in school.

FACT OR FICTION?

Leo Tolstoy graduated from college with honors and won the Nobel Prize for literature.

FICTION !

This great author of WAR AND PEACE left college without graduating. His books were nominated ten times for the Nobel Prize for Literature but he never won it. Other authors who did win during those years are forgotten today. Tolstoy's work lives on!

FACT OR FICTION?

Six publishers turned down Beatrix Potter's PETER RABBIT.

FACT !

Six publishers did think that a story about a silly little rabbit who gets in trouble in a garden would never sell. The author of PETER RABBIT, Beatrix Potter, was not discouraged. She used her own money to have the book published.

FACT OR FICTION?

Sarah Bernhardt showed early talent as an actress.

FICTION !

A"Who would have imagined it?" Sarah's aunt exclaimed as she admired Sarah's books and paintings. "When I found her as an abandoned and starving child, I had no idea there was such talent in those thin bones."
Sarah's aunt, who surely saved her from an early death, lived to see the child grow up to become first a painter, then a writer and finally one of the greatest actresses the world has ever known.

FACT OR FICTION?

George Gershwin hated music.

FACT!

"Hands are for fighting, not for playing a sissy piano," George shouted. He knew you had to be tough to survive in his neighborhood. Until, of course, the day he heard Maxie!

Maxie played the violin. He played the most beautiful music George had ever heard. George had to know how such music could be! He and Maxie became friends and George put as much energy into making music as he had in creating bloody noses. His rare and beautiful music is enjoyed all over the world today.

Gifted or Goof-Off?

Talented people don't always show their gifts early in life! Rudyard Kipling, Noel Coward, Mark Twain and Charles Dickens never finished grade school!

Here is a light-hearted look at the early lives of some very gifted and talented people. You decide!

➥ Fact or Fiction? ↩

- Hans Christian Andersen couldn't spell.
- Thomas Edison was a firebug.
- Charles Lindbergh was afraid of heights.
- Louisa May Alcott wrote shocking books.
- Einstein spoke at six months.
- Grandma Moses never had an art lesson.
- Alexander Graham Bell never finished a project.

You'll discover the fact or fiction about these gifted people and more in HANS CHRISTIAN ANDERSEN COULDN'T SPELL!

P. O. Box 9450
O'Fallon, MO
63366

ISBN 0-913839-67-1